Ripples in Tranquil Waters

Published by
Lotus Press Publishers & Distributors

Ripples in Tranquil Waters

Ankur Dang

Lotus PRESS

4735/22, Prakash Deep Building,
Ansari Road, Dariyaganj,
New Delhi - 110002

Lotus Press Publishers & Distributors
Unit No. 220, Second Floor, 4735/22, Prakash Deep Building,
Ansari Road, Darya Ganj, New Delhi-110002
Ph.: 011-23280047, 32903912
E-mail: lotuspress1984@gmail.com
www.lotuspress.co.in

Ripples in Tranquil Waters

ISBN: 978-81-8382-312-8
Cover Designed by Binay Dimri

Published by: **Lotus Press Publishers & Distributors** New Delhi - 110002

Preface

Human life is a complex and Colorful joyride of a multitude of experiences. Through our years of physical and spiritual growth, we learn the serenity of pain and the fickleness of pleasure. However, some of the most poignant of these emotions find their free expression within the rhythms of poetry. In my journey from carefree childhood to liberated youth, life has revealed itself to me in its numerous shades, both delightful and dark. 'Ripples in tranquil waters' is a broken tale of completion told through the medium of verse. It is a piece of my soul that I am sharing with you as I celebrate life and its ups and downs. Feel free to share your thoughts with me at ankurdang93@gmail.com.

–Author

Dedicated to

my parents, whose

love keeps me strong

Contents

Preface • (v)

•

An Echo in the Forest of Holy Basil • 11

Being a Man • 12

Saying Goodbye • 15

A Grave of your Digging • 17

Closure • 19

In the Memory of Alina • 21

Deliverance • 23

Have you seen my lost little heart? • 24

I wish I were your Mother • 26

Lady Grace • 28

Mariam • 30

On Loss and Healing • 31

Outpour • 34

She • 35

So Sings Raavi • 37

Death of a Song • 40

The Lament of Thanatos • 42

The Martyr's Wife • 44

The other Woman • 47

Village Girl • 49

To God and to Man • 51

To Ma, with Love • 53

To my Savior • 56

Departure • 58

Call of Humanity • 59

Ghost Child • 60

An Empty Park • 61

Muses of a Dream Come True • 62

Calling Nanna • 63

Queen • 64

The Robber • 65

Paradise • 67

The Playdate • 69

M'esmerelda • 71

The Hero • 72

An Echo in the Forest of Holy Basil

●

O the Lord of my heart,
I thirst for a glimpse of thee...
The shadows dance in her austere hut,
as Meera chants thy name in yearning.
The weeds of words are plenty here....
but not one flower,
worthy so to be blessed
in thy sweet remembrance.
Meera sings and whirls,
in the forest of holy basil....
Ecstatic, lunatic, a Radhika Reborn.....
Meera dances to thy flute.
Grace her being with red,
the hue of one eternally wed.
Give me but one glimpse of thee
and in my love, O divine one,
set thy Meera free.

• • •

Being a Man

●

What does it take to be a man,
true to his word and name....
Does it take the glory of war or
the pseudo wealth of fame....

How different are his mind and heart,
that distinguish him from the rest....
What makes him the king of hearts of men,
and better than the best....

What hot sands have burnt his feet,
which though pierced by thorns, feel no pain....
What fires his blood and makes it flow,
free and wild, breaking all chains....

What is it that was never seen,
and yet does express in his dreams....
A rugged man he is,
and has been everywhere, it seems....

But what is it that preserves his soul,
as it was the day he was born....
A sacred thread around his being,
since that day he has worn....

A thread of truth and justice,
that gives him the courage to fight....
To stand firm in faith and walk the path,
that leads him to what is right....

Such a man needs no honour,
from a world that can't see beyond....
His power is his belief, and his love,
which keeps him strong....

Such a man fears no agony,
no torment nor the blackness of death....
His life is a life lived for others,
and for justice till his last breath....

This man will die a mortal but
will be proud to have truly lived....
For what is life in which,
one had nothing to die for and nothing to give....

He shall seek no mercy in this material world,
no matter the price of his pride....
A man of truth wouldn't bend to wrong,
with his God on his side....

His virtue would be the salt of the earth,
and in his endeavor he would succeed....
He would nourish the earth back to life,
with every wound of his that'd bleed....

Standing alone yet not so,
he is a man who'd never quit or flee....
You can break his body but not his spirit,
he was born free and will always be....

• • •

Saying Goodbye

I know what you're going to say,
It is too far now to come back this way.

Just this once, Love, hear me out,
Hear my tender command and turn around.

There is still so much left to know,
Don't you think it was too soon to go.

The folks are waiting outside for you,
How can I break their trust so true?

I stand empty here, so cold and alone,
Did you lie all along or had you just not known?

The pain is so much; my well of tears runs dry,
There is nothing to do but to hold myself and cry.

Your memories scorch and soothe all the same,
Are we no longer 'us' or we still do have a name?

How do I say sorry and how do I forgive you?
You made a million vows but kept just so few.

'Hear me now love, and let your grief flow,
I stand here beside you without letting you know.

There is the pearl I held so dear,
Our shared smile and your lonesome tear.

Hold me now and my presence feel,
Forget me not but let go and heal.

Let the rain fall and wash the hurt away,
I did never leave because in your heart I stay.

• • •

A Grave of your Digging

●

Can you feel this pain so close,
like its throbbing in your veins,
coursing through like blood,
as it leaves you black and stained.

Can you feel this pain so close,
as they chain you by your heart.
They strip you down and flog you,
then they stake you with that dart.

Can you feel this pain so close,
as you cry for a mercy that's dead.
Your naked body crumbles to naught
but your dust is tinted red.

Can you feel this pain so close;
as for respite, you cry and howl.
They won't listen, they mock you,
you are tainted, you're foul.

Can you feel this pain so close,
as you see the shell you've become.
Do you know, this is nemesis?
your gift for what you've done.

Can you feel this pain so close.
I bet you can feel it raw.
It has finally come for you,
Injustice was your fatal flaw.

• • •

Closure

As the seasons have come and gone,
I have seen the air turn rose and azure,
I have seen it through my soul....
The night, Slowly as it spreads
its dark and lovely brilliance,
in a moment, the black gives way to the white.
I have felt it....

The shudder of a leaf as it sways,
to the slow dance of the wind,
the smile of a baby as it dreams,
of meadows of joy, in its sleep....
the song of the river as it gently serenades,
the lonely bird at night....
I have touched it....

Lives stripped from a people,
and the love held in the mist,
at the grave of those united only in death....,
Of those who met never yet met for eternity....
And that which I have seen and won't see again !
Yes, I have seen it....

The soft patter of the rain at my window,
The warmth of the winter sun,
as it comforts my cold flesh....
The purity of the snow,
as it melts into the ground....
I have known it....

I have tasted each sensation,
as it has swirled around me and past me,
to touch another soul and open its eyes,
to bless it with a view the colorful world,
otherwise closed to it forever....
To soothe the heartache
for a glimpse of what I would never see.

I am blessed in each little sigh,
I am fortunate in the autumns of life....
In hatred I found unconditional love.
I wept....
For joy, and found it!

• • •

In the Memory of Alina

•

Alina, Alina
Why did you go away?
Alina, Alina
Was it so hard to stay?

Alina, Alina
What about your dreams?
Alina, Alina
Can you hear my screams?

Alina, Alina
Can you hear what I say?
Alina, Alina
Please give me just today?

Alina, Alina
Are you in much pain?
Alina, Alina
Was our friendship in vain?

Alina, Alina
Will you come back?
Alina, Alina
Will our memories go black?

Alina, Alina
Will you wait for me?
Alina, Alina
Will we someday be free?

Alina, Alina
This is a passing curtain.
Alina, Alina
I will see you again....

Dedicated to Alina Procopiescu,
a dear friend and a wonderful human being.

• • •

Deliverance

●

My words flow forth, not worthy of thee....
O you, the cherished one....
Sustain me this day, pardon my sin....
Those of a faithful transgressor.

I know not of your highness, nor who you be....
but I heard them call you 'Raheem'....
Grant me mercy, just this last once;
To an Incoherent lowborn beggar.

I am alone, drifting along in this sea....
Please be my anchor I pray....
Take me home, I'm tired and sick;
Make me your lost child found.

• • •

Have you seen my lost little heart?

Have you seen my lost little heart?
I lost it early that morn....
I followed fast when I jumped with a start,
as I heard the strange strain of a horn.

Have you seen my lost little heart?
I lost it while playing in the wood....
I muddied my clothes, once so smart,
as I played with a friend from my childhood.

Have you seen my lost little heart,
I can't seem to find it anywhere....
oh, he must have taken it in his toy cart;
stolen from me and hidden somewhere.

Have you seen my lost little heart?
or even my lost little lover....
Ask him to come back if you saw him depart,
Tell him, I found the nest of a plover.

Have you seen my lost little heart?
I've grown old without it you know....
I've lived as a shell for the most part,
But I must let my grief now flow.

If you see my lost little heart,
please leave it under a bush or a tree....
It might be hurt or even torn apart,
but its dead and no use to me.

• • •

I wish I were your Mother

I wish I were your mother,
to share my love with you....
It's hard to kiss you to sleep,
And not have you know it too....

I wish I were your mother,
to hold you close to my heart....
I have so much to say to you,
But I don't know where to start.

I wish I were your mother,
So I could see your sunny smile.
I can only wish from a distance,
for I'm yours, but you're not mine.

I wish I were your mother,
So I could feed you with my hands....
I wish I had been blessed so,
to see your first footprints in sand.

I wish I were your mother,
So you could share your grief with me,
But may you never feel such need,
For your dream catcher, I will be.

I wish I were your mother,
This emptiness is wild....
Sometimes, it lies beside me,
Like a little newborn child.

I wish I were your mother,
It was my wish upon a star....
It didn't quite come true but,
It let me be your angel from afar....

Dedicated to children living in foster homes and orphanages across the world; some of whom I met in Romania and who taught me that life isn't about finding shelter in the storm, it is about dancing in the rain and loving every moment of it.

• • •

Lady Grace

●

Lady Grace, so young yet wise;
Why the faraway haze in your eyes?

Lady Grace, so serene and sedate;
Why leave your palm in the hands of fate?

Lady Grace, this pain in your heart;
Why not let it go and make a new start?

Lady Grace, these broken dreams;
Why not let me silence those screams?

Lady Grace, this blood on your wrists;
Why drain your life away for heavenly mists?

Lady Grace, forever hurt and alone;
Why no fear of the untouched, unknown?

Lady Grace, taking stone breaths?
Why die each moment a thousand deaths?

Lady Grace, forever sharp and knowing;
Why so restless with your heartbeat slowing?

Lady Grace, so lovely and dear;
Why did you leave, or are you still here?

Lady Grace, your funeral song;
"I found my place, this is where I belong"

• • •

Mariam

Eyes shut in prayer,
hands folded in a plea....
on her knees to wait,
for the blessings of her lord.
Blessed light of the mountain,
beneathe her feet, soft grass....
and a veil of soft silk,
covers her serene face.
she knows he will be gifted,
the king of kings among men.
the generous angel of healing
with powers to raise the dead.
born to her, whose soul is pure,
whose body is clean....
and the prophet prince grows,
in the womb of blessed mariam.

• • •

On Loss and Healing

•

Have you seen an old woman
with cold and sad, wet eyes?
She hasn't spoken a word till now
but have you heard her silent cries?

Do you know , what has caused her sorrow?
It is the death of her precious child
She looks longingly at the day after tomorrow
which died , before it could be alive.

Her son was the apple of her eye
He was a child in the midst of his prime
but what caused his life to fade away?
Why did his flame extinguish before time?

You now know why she's so sad
You whisper as you pass her by
She looks at the world, which seems so bad
and she quietly walks away, no longer crying.

You have been invited to the funeral
She's your neighbour , so you decide to go
but as soon as the pyre's lit,
you decide to go back and stay no more.

You see her around sometimes
but you're scared of saying even 'hi'
You hurriedly smile and move out of her sight
Should she talk of her son and cry.

You don't talk to her, though you want to know
what exactly happened to her son
But you say to yourself-' It's not right,
It would cause her pain and that's not done.'

But you don't realise, what you can do
when her heart is so full of grief
Open up yours, so sincere and true
to give her a reason to smile again and heal.

Its these little things that matter a lot
a thoughful blessing , put in during prayer
or on a cold, wet night, a meal kept hot
To let her know that you care.

You try and start a conversation
and just like that, you talk to her
You cry with her over some old memories
and laugh out loud at the others.

We so often assume too much
and forget what kind words can do
We underestimate the power of love
and we forget, that's the only thing that's true.

A little call can make such a big difference
or a casual-' let's go for lunch together'
warm her heart and let her smile with you
as you replace her thorns with heather.

You don't really need to go out of your way
just keep close and let her know that you care
cause ultimately, all that matters is
that when she needed you, you were there....

It isn't too much to ask for,
And it isn't too much to give.
One day you will be dead and gone,
But your love shall forever live.

• • •

Outpour

•

The dying embers of passion stir within me,
My aged beauty longs to charm again.
It yearns for the timelessness to be,
as it searches for a reality long undone.

The blood in my marrow boils with my need,
To be held and loved and fawned over.
I cry over my crinkled reflection; I bleed,
for one more moment of my long ended reign.

The memoirs of touch linger still on my skin,
like love poetry written on old parchment.
The smell of cheap smoke and nightly sin;
My sagging breasts mock the lady in the mirror.

My palace of ill repute is a macabre untruth,
without the patrons with their sly smiles.
But I know the fickle faithfulness of youth,
Alas, it seeks not to please but to destroy.

I lie alone with tales of depravity and pleasure,
Lamenting a destiny I wrote with my pain.
Maybe someone will come searching at leisure,
The lost treasure of an old harlot's heart.

• • •

She

•

The soul of a woman, encased in green....

The misty crystal, with a faint, faded sheen....

With silent tears that fail to cease,

The hem of her veil fluttering in the breeze....

Her short quick steps and the furrowed brow,

Her gaze is lowered and her head is bowed.

Her belief in her faith, strengthens her to endure,

She is passionate in love but unhappy yet pure....

She has no name, no face, no choice....

Tolerance is her weapon, her silence her voice....

She is your sister, your daughter, your wife,

She has submitted so long but with grace, all her life....

Her nights know the pain of each blow you dealt to her,

She is waiting for the end, to sicken away, to wither....

The only joy she has known, is the pride of Motherhood,

In spite of all your curses, that one ground she has stood....

'forsaken....forsaken' destiny screams....

But what more can shatter, after her dead dreams.

She smiles at her fate, and mocks it too....

Who is anyone to decide, her own vice and virtue!

Now she is lying still, awaiting dawn....

And lo, comes light....She is gone!

• • •

Human History is a complex and intricate mural of many colors and images. These images are tinted with both; the blue of hope and the red of blood, these images are the story of the human mind and the silent spectator called nature. Here is the story of 'Raavi', one of the five rivers of Punjab, as she sings her heart out with pain and sorrow, at the 1947 partition of India, one of the biggest migrations in history. Nearly 2 million people lost their lives in this bloodbath and 17 million people fled from their homes in their bid to survive the flames of this human inferno.

So Sings Raavi

•

The crystal color of my being,
stands still in the streams of time.
I see through the aging shadows,
I see memories in their prime.

Raavi ve, O Raavi,
See the lines drawn in sand,
Don't laugh or cry, Sweet mother,
It's the fate of the human hand.

I rush through the pebbled pathways,
to reach my beloved fields of Punjab.
But Oh !this heat of searing blood,
strains of agony play the *Rubab.*

Raavi ve, O Raavi,
See the lines drawn in sand,
Don't laugh or cry, Sweet mother,
It's the fate of the human hand.

I am undeterred by your fences,
I am free to choose my course.
Why, O Son, you forget then,
I am an element of your life force.

Raavi ve, O Raavi,
See the lines drawn in sand,
Don't laugh or cry, Sweet mother,
It's the fate of the human hand.

I have kissed the mists of the past;
I have held history in my arms,
I have known the cries of your hatred,
I have seen death in your farms.

Raavi ve, O Raavi,
See the lines drawn in sand,
Don't laugh or cry, Sweet mother,
It's the fate of the human hand.

I have little to say to you,
You are an ancient river man,
But save your boat from burning,
Steer it far away, if you can.

Raavi ve, O Raavi,
See the lines drawn in sand,
Don't laugh or cry, Sweet mother,
It's the fate of the human hand.

I cry alone and for no one,
I regret, I atone, I repent.
I couldn't save my dear home;
So Five lone rivers lament....

• • •

Death of a Song

Music , as thy memory,
Echoes in my heart....
Roses dried and dead....
Spines like aimed darts....

The merry world around me,
Crumbles away into dust....
The last of the wine of love,
The last of the words of trust....

My eyes are closed and hands open,
What have I left but a memory of love....
And that, which we built together,
Now away it has flown, to the skies above....

They say thy eyes see all and none....
Can thee see my soul, now dead?
Can thee see what thy loss has done?
And my blood, no longer red....

Will there be back to soothe my ache?
They say I'm hurt and time shall heal,
But what when a part of me is dead....
And nothing I see and nothing I feel....

I shall not bother thee anymore,
I prayed each day for thy pain to cease....
I shall be gone forever more,
And in death I know, I will find my peace....

• • •

The Lament of Thanatos

•

The storm is sweeping,
across the plains....
Will it also wipe way,
These old blood stains?

The sounds of the last battle,
are music to my stone ears
The thick pain of despair,
To my soul is so dear.

I am,
Alone, unloved, Unclaimed,
I am,
A force, uncontrolled, unchained.

I am destruction, lethal and sure,
I am walking death with no cure.
I am mercy, cold and just,
I am justice, where I must.
I am the wind that whistles sharp.
I am the star that glows in the dark.

I am the pearl that fell from an eye.
I am the last cloud in a stormy sky.
I was fashioned from the clay of grief.
I am now, a long forgotten memory.
I am the ghost that haunts your dreams.
I am the pure, untouched crystal stream.
I am your laughter, your smile and your tear.
I am your victory and also your fear.

I am,
Alone, unloved, Unclaimed,
I am,
A force, uncontrolled, unchained.

The sounds of the last battle,
numbed me to that pain.
My Agony soothes my mind,
So I don't hear the melancholy strains

The storm is sweeping,
Across the plains.
Will it also wipe away,
These old blood stains.

• • •

The Martyr's Wife

The whispers of the wind tell me a tale....
A tale I know as the melody of my voice;
The last dust crumbles in my hands,
I hear my life cry and my destiny rejoice.

I have yearned for so long and with no true ends,
to see him be once or be born again,
I have shivered in the cold and felt the warmth,
I have touched the dew and drenched in the rain.

I waited each day and night through the battle cries,
I walked so fast and yet it was too late!
Was it so destined that nothing could've been done?
A strange belief in hope and a strange fear of fate?

To the Master, you pledged your loyalty,
To me you gave your soul....
To your men, you gave your honor and blood,
And all to the Father who made you whole.

And now you are complete,
I see your eyes at ease,
Your silent song sounds sweet,
And your still hair dance through the breeze....

It is coming; I can feel the chill in the air,
their eyes are sharp and their minds are ready....
Its over before it has begun and they know it
Still they don't shiver, and their hands are so steady !

I hear him too, the one of my heart....
He stands with them, will stand till the last....
I fear the end, I cherish the beginning,
I look to our motherland and skies so vast.

And that's all that's left of him to the world,
But to me, he's here, who wasn't ever gone.
The night is cool and his touch is pleasant....
An eternity of joy as it approaches dawn....

They say I'm young and pretty and fair....
Why must I live a life that's torn....?
Tell them I am his queen, his beloved one,
And his love, around my being I've worn.

And the vows were meant, when our blood we joined.
The kiss still lingers, moist and deep....
The room is chilled and I shiver at times....
As you slowly leave as I cry for sleep....

Long after now, you'll always still be there,
Will you be back to hug your bird?
Your sugar plum, your beautiful one,
The one you loved, with so much more than just words.

I shall wait, with my arms open to you,
For a last embrace, to soothe my aching heart....
I wait for you still, my cherished one....
Death shall not do us apart....

• • •

The other Woman

•

Don't call me by that name;
Don't say I ruined your life.
I am human too, you see,
even though I am not the wife.

Ungodly, loose, characterless;
My unholy descriptions have no end.
The other woman; that's me,
I borrowed what wasn't to lend.

Your man was never mine;
I made no false claims over him.
I shared his pain in your absence,
I just lit up his eyes so dim.

It wasn't that you were lacking;
No, he didn't mean to hurt you.
But fate was mean to you and me,
for loves that were both true.

His guilt for your pain is immense;
His heart is burdened forever.
For an escape in his weakest hour,
He just couldn't his ties sever.

But now Sister, hear me out;
He is and will only be yours.
Scream, rage and shout but,
remember, it is you he adores.

I was but a passing phase;
an echo of a summer breeze.
Hold him close to you now,
Hear the song of happy trees.

I won't return to walk this path;
I have found my strength in your smile.
Don't hate me please, is all I ask,
Let me walk in peace this last mile.

• • •

Village Girl

●

Her bundle is heavy,
as she treks through the forest;
Her veil hides her laughter
even as her musical echo is heard.
On the stony paths to the village,
She walks with her anklets jingling,
The bells, all together delight,
In their happy chorus of a joyful new bride.
Her simple smile is radiant,
even devoid of its *shringaar.*
Her bangles shimmer
in the morning sun,
glorious as the vermillion,
honored at the seat of her soul.

The happy chatter of household matters,
Of mothers and in-laws alike,
Of lazy children and lazy husbands,
And of things of her own dislike.
The pitchers of water,
The jars of home-made butter,
The cry of the old rooster;
Are the pride of her heart.
Don't ridicule this *dehati* girl,
'who knows nothing';
She is the salt of the earth,
With her place in the stars.

• • •

To God and to Man

•

When I'm dying, My Lord,
Let my hand be in yours.
Bury my sins with me, My Friends,
And give my soul to God.

Don't miss me, when I'm no longer there
Don't cry over my dead form
Remember the good deeds, I may have done
And forgive me for my wrongs.

Give my eyes to a blind man
So that he may see the colours of love
Give my heart to a dying child
At whom I'll smile from above.

Give my virtues to satan
So that his soul may also be pure
Give my vices to an angel
Because I know, my soul, he'll cure.

Give my blood in sacrifice
And with it, wash the sacred earth
May my ashes nourish the crops
And may no one know any dearth.

Burn me in the holy fire
And let my ego melt away
Let my arrogance die
and let me be re-born, this day.

Remember my memories, when I'm gone
And keep me close to your heart
But don't count your breaths in mine
Because to unite in death; in life, we part.

When I'm dying, My Lord
Let my hand be in yours
See me through till the end
As I enter thy heavenly abode.

• • •

To Ma, with Love

It's been four years now,
and it's still so hard to say....
Every moment of that day,
seems just as alive as today....

The waiting, the hoping,
the praying and the tears....
The dread, the despair,
the distress and the fear....

We knew it'd end but,
which way we hadn't known....
You left us grieving as one,
but standing all alone....

We wondered if you'd be back,
but to the ashes you had turned....
your presence in your absence,
like the incense of mourning burned....

All over our home,
were the imprints of your hands....
but your memories were slipping fast,
like the sea-shore sands....

"Why so soon?" we asked you,
but you never did reply....
And sometimes, even the pain would go,
and leave the numbness to die....

Then once I asked dad,
if you could see me grow and hear me talk....
He put his arm around me and
took me with himself for a walk....

He said–"look in to the heavens,
the skies so far above,–
Ma is now with the angels and
she's blessing you with her love"

I still do miss you sometimes,
and wish you'd still be here....
but papa said that no matter what,
you are always near....

I don't know what happens once we die
but here is a promise I want from you....
If I do my best to find you,
then you must do it too....

I know we'll be together again and
there's so much I need you to know....
We'll talk and laugh like the old
times and never again let go....

I was never the perfect daughter and
of my duties I had no clue....
But even then, I want you to know,
I love you and will always do....

• • •

To my Savior

•

Hold me tight, just hold me once....
Don't leave me here, don't push me around....
I'm tired, alone, spent and hurt....
Hold me forever for I have been found....

You have seen my tears and heard my cries,
You ask me why I lower my gaze,
Why I look away and avert my lovely eyes....
Can you show me what you see as you clear my haze?

Your touch feels so soft, so gentle and warm,
so sure and strong, so close and true....
You calm my fears, the raging storms....
Is this my deliverance, this faith so new....

I ask you 'why' and you kiss my hand....
I ask you 'where' and you tell me you're here....
I ask you not a word but you still understand,
When I cry in my sleep, I still find you near.

I feel I'm dead, unworthy, unclean....
You say I'm alive and pure and complete,
I pull my veil closer, I mustn't be seen....
You reveal my face again and let our eyes meet....

I don't feel real, I'm too sick at heart,
But you still do believe that I'm not gone....
You look for the lost me, the one torn apart,
You believe in life and the coming dawn.

You are stubborn, in your faith in me....
I am amazed, but I'm secretly glad,
I want to live again, I was born free....
you want my passion, positive and mad.

It isn't that simple but you knew it always,
It wasn't my fault , you knew that too....
I couldn't talk, as shame consumed my days....
And the shadows so filthy, but now it's just you.

He broke my body but not my soul....
The scars will stay but not for long....
I will heal because I'm forever yours,
This is me, an unchained song....

• • •

Departure

●

I walk along the cobbled street,
with little slips of paper in hand.
I hum a sad little song to myself,
by some old, forgotten band.

Your old love letters are all still there,
filled with adoring words so sweet.
The fragrant smell of an old perfume,
lingers in the yellowing sheets.

The old wine from some mountain hamlet,
The pitter-patter of mid-summer rains;
How rich is the song of the nightingale,
The melody of a love lost to pain.

I paint the dreary walls of my heart,
with colors of a time gone by.
Don't come back to me, O dear one,
Let this last time be goodbye.

• • •

Call of Humanity

A rush of wings,

In a mellow wind;

The joy gushes out,

as a stream of memories.

The waterfall of my tears,

Of happy faith;

Ecstatic in the whirl

of a dervishes' dance.

They hold my hand,

reach out to me,

to set me free,

to let me be...

• • •

Ghost Child

•

A cot stands beside the white wall;
In a nursery strangely quiet.
No healthy infant wails for milk,
No innocent laughter causes a riot.

No nurse awaits the arrival of,
Children coming back from play.
No waiting mother guides smilingly,
a child who has lost his way.

A tap-tap caused by little feet,
disturbs the still and silent backyard.
A gurgling giggle escapes her lips,
A smile lights up her face so scarred

She calls you to join her game,
She is bored of playing all alone.
A hundred years is a long time,
for even a memory cast in stone.

Nobody knows this unnamed girl,
this creature so serene and mild.
But this is her home and play-ground,
for she is just a lost ghost child.

• • •

An Empty Park

•

O Call upon the love of mothers,

and the winds of joy of old....

Where, O where are the children,

Whose tales of play were told,

to the children of today;

more somber than the last man on the post....

The eyes of laughter are sunken,

in meadows of flowery ghosts....

One tiny upturned lip,

lo, the heart of joy soars,

in the hope of beauty returning,

with children back in the park....

• • •

Muses of a Dream Come True

•

Summer dream, an endless chain....

Of thoughts and wishes,

Unsaid, unheard....

Unknown, Unhurt....

Break the chain, see what you've found.

Behold the world in your palm....

Let time's sand not pass you by....

By you,

Untouched, Unmarked....

• • •

Calling Nanna

•

A new breath of air,
Spiced with cinnamon and home;
The little box with tiny beads,
The parka with polka dots;
Old grandma's last gift....
The touch of her wrinkled hands,
of an ancient, gnarled tree.
The warm comfort of a petting lullaby;
This forgotten childhood song, Ah....

The shuffling of feet in the dead of the night,
The morning sun still rises with her chants....
Make me a home in your heart, Old Mother,
Give me a place in your wizened soul.
I know your spirit roams free,
Like the essence of your stories;
Let the thirsty crow be me!

• • •

Queen

•

I clutched my doll like a lifeline,
When I came to a lonely road,
Till big strong hands picked me up,
and took me home as it snowed.

The hard hands shaped by toil,
with the love of a father's heart,
held mine close and wiped my tears
as the shadows grew big in the dark.

The wishes were given in heirlooms,
to the heiress of numerous dreams,
as the little princess ascended the throne,
rising from a lovely, rose hued stream.

The strong hand held her gentle one,
As she walked the aisle in her veil,
He squeezed her hand and calmed her fears,
As he today, gave her away.

Pearls shimmered in the misty eyes,
of an aged man and a youthful girl,
from a child queen, to a queen of hearts,
His daughter was all his world.

• • •

The Robber

Through tiresome hungry nights,
The silver moon looks on.
My blade shines in the dark,
Unafraid of the impending dawn.

The travelling bands of broken men,
Hike wearily to find their home.
I wait in the shadows of an old pine,
Biding my time as they roam.

Their merry stories reek to high heaven,
Of their unwashed bodies and hearts.
With shattered destinies to mend,
Once again on their mission they start.

They talk of faraway lands and tales,
Of fair people I shall never see.
But I weave a tapestry of images,
Painted in colors glorious and free.

I should like to listen some more,
To know these 'almost friends'.
But I know the time is near,
When means must lead to ends.

Lithe as the panther of the moon,
I strike; and they cower in fear.
I proudly take my spoils of victory,
And leave them dead, but dear.

And a haunting hum finds my lips,
'almost friends', I feel remorse.
But today we shall eat a bellyful,
And not worry about the source.

When the morrow comes I will cry,
At the last lost chance for peace.
Redemption comes easy to a soul,
But not to soulless ones like me.

• • •

Paradise

●

The scents of autumn greet me,
As I think back to the home of my fathers.
The green and golden apple tree,
with its rich bounty weighing it down......
The lush valleys tug at my homesick heart,
They call upon the echoes of my childhood.
Further ahead, I greet a rivulet,
onits way to join its big brother.
The warm sun smiles pleasantly
at this picture of otherworldly grandeur;
The holy mother holds her head high,
as she blesses her children of the soil.
Her mighty crown of both clouds and winds,
commands all creation to sing for joy.
The sweet earth joins in the serenade,
As a linnet finds its rightful place,
in a song of infinite harmonies.

My astral travel ends... Alas;
The crescendo reaches the heavens above.
The chill of snow is felt closer;
With autumn's warm smile waning.
The linnet breaks into a solo;
even though spring seems far still.
But the dancing colors in this kaleidoscope,
Foretell the coming of flowers again.
Let us rejoice.......
Let us rejoice.......

• • •

The Playdate

It was a cold and foggy morning,
My weekly playdate with a friend.
I parked my car in the driveway,
Familiar with the ritualistic trend.

I picked her favorite lilies, white;
And walked slowly to where we'd meet.
The little path, flanked by flowers,
Looked pretty and smelled sweet.

Deeply enjoying my leisurely stroll,
Soon I reached my destination.
I lay the flowers on the ground,
At the foot of her final station.

I kissed the cold surface thrice,
The way I did whenever alone.
What should have been warm flesh,
Was nothing but a tombstone.

I sat in her presence for a while,
Till I noticed a forgotten grave.
Curious, I approached it carefully,
Wishing desperately to be brave.

"Here lies ol' unwanted Johnny,
Who died wi' a guitar in hand.
sang songs to the deaf and dumb;
Yon crazy one man band"

A faded card lay a few feet away,
'from deaf fans, to our Rock star';
Who was anyone to write his epitaph,
When his voice had reached that far.

No intense emotion clutched my heart,
No fat tears rolled down my face,
Old Johnny had been a merry man,
But he had gotten his tribute and grace.

A smile stole its way onto my lips,
Old Johnny's unheard song I knew,
My lilies called me to the other grave,
And they were covered in dew.

• • •

M'esmerelda

•

The quiet steps grace the air,
As the floor comes alive,
with a fine subtle rhythm.
The mauve lace on a tiny shoe,
Stands still in mid arch.....
Of feet poised so gaily.
An aria of love lost finds voice,
In her arms held aloft.
She sways to the melody,
Drinking in adulation.
'*M'esmerelda*', they whisper,
Behind Lady Enigma,
As she charms her way,
To fame........
To fortune.........
Through magic........
Of just her dancing feet.

• • •

The Hero

O dear mother, you are freedom;
Hear the strains of the last post.
Your son was a soldier brave,
To his spirit, let us raise a toast.

He soldiered on in the dark,
in sleet and snow and storms.
His didn't find his aura in war,
But in the lives he helped transform.

He didn't teach them to read,
He didn't give them a sermon of life.
But he aided their solitary escape,
He gave them the chance to survive;

To kids trapped in mud trenches,
To eyes horrified and moist,
To unlit fires in empty hearths,
To uncertain fears unvoiced.